BAGDASARIAN
PRODUCTIONS

ALVINNN!!!
AND THE CHIPMUNKS™
Simon in Charge!

based on the screenplay "To Serve and Protect"
written by Janice Karman
adapted by Lauren Forte

Ready-to-Read

Simon Spotlight

New York　　London　　Toronto　　Sydney　　New Delhi

SIMON SPOTLIGHT
An imprint of Simon & Schuster Children's Publishing Division
1230 Avenue of the Americas, New York, New York 10020
This Simon Spotlight edition July 2018
Alvin and The Chipmunks, The Chipettes and Characters TM & © 2018 Bagdasarian
Productions, LLC. All Rights Reserved. Agent: PGS USA
For information about special discounts for bulk purchases, please contact
Simon & Schuster Special Sales at 1-866-506-1949 or business@simonandschuster.com.
Manufactured in the United States of America 0518 LAK
10 9 8 7 6 5 4 3 2 1
ISBN 978-1-5344-1630-7 (hc)
ISBN 978-1-5344-1629-1 (pbk)
ISBN 978-1-5344-1631-4 (eBook)

"I'm the new safety monitor at school!" Simon said excitedly as he ran into the kitchen.

"You've told us a thousand times," complained Alvin.

"What do you have to do, Simon?" Dave asked.

"If someone is loitering, I give them a ticket," Simon answered. "Or if someone is littering, another ticket. I am the eyes and ears of the teachers when they are not there."

"Simon is basically the school snitch. It's a supercool job," Alvin said sarcastically. "Now let's talk about vacation!"

"Hold on! Before we see which dream vacation we take this year, let's go over the rules," declared Dave.
"Ugh," Alvin groaned.

Simon quickly spoke up. "The week before our trip, we must do all our chores. And if we have problems, we work them out ourselves."

"We don't bother you," Theodore said to Dave.
"And if one of us gets in trouble that week, the trip is off," Alvin finished.

Dave held out three straws. "Okay, whoever gets the longest straw picks our vacation spot." "I've won the last three," Alvin bragged. "I'm going to win again."

But Simon got the longest straw! "Where do you want to go, Simon?" Dave asked.

"I've been waiting to pick this straw forever," Simon gushed. "The Smithsonian. It's like ten museums in one!"

Alvin was really unhappy.
"I can't go there!" he said.
"Those places make me all tired.
I can't do it! Simon, please pick
another place! Please!"

"I'm sorry, Alvin," Simon answered. "I've been dying to see the Smithsonian. Maybe you will find it interesting."

In school that day, Simon was taking his job as safety supervisor very seriously. He handed out tickets to kids as they littered, or if they stayed in the hallway after the bell.

Alvin faked a stomachache and asked his teacher, Mrs. Smith, if he could use the bathroom. But when he got into the hallway, he sat down to read a comic book.

"Alvin! What are you doing?" Simon asked as he passed him.
"Just relaxing, reading a comic book," Alvin responded.

"You have to go back to class," Simon warned. "I'll have to write you a ticket if you don't."

"Oh, really," Alvin said with a giggle. "If I get in trouble, then nooo Smithsonian. . . ."

Simon took out his ticket book.
He started to write a ticket
but then stopped. He couldn't
bring himself to do it.

The next day as Simon patrolled the halls, he saw some boys fooling around. But when he handed them a ticket, one of them shouted, "Hey, you can't give us a ticket if you didn't give your brother one!"

Simon was frustrated.
He stopped giving out tickets,
even though some kids really
deserved them.

Someone *really* deserved one.

Later, at home, Simon and Alvin were fighting. They pretended everything was fine the minute Dave walked into the room.

Alvin even refused to clean his room, which was one of his chores! Simon did it for him because he didn't want to risk anyone getting in trouble and having the trip canceled.

The next morning Alvin waited for
Simon as he left the safety office.
"Oh no! You caught me!"
Alvin teased. "Are you going to
give me a ticket?"

"No, I'm not," Simon responded. "I turned in my badge. I'm not fit to wear it. And when I tell Dave we've been fighting, I'm sure the trip will be off as well. So you win."

Alvin felt terrible.

"Wait, Simon! But you always wanted to be the safety thing . . . and the trip . . ."

But Simon walked away sadly.

Alvin knew he needed to fix things.

At home later that afternoon, Alvin put the safety badge back on Simon's shirt and said, "You deserve this more than anyone I know."
"What?!" Simon yelled.

"I told Dave everything," Alvin said. "Well, not everything. But you're still going to the Smithsonian! And the best part? I don't have to go! I'll just stay with someone else."
"It's a punishment, Alvin!" Dave called from the other room.

And, true to Dave's word, Alvin stayed with his teacher, Mrs. Smith.

"I see the Smithsonian has an exhibition on the history of surfboards this week," Mrs. Smith said.

"What?" Alvin cried. He *loved* surfing. "Kelly Slater, the famous surfer, is going to be there to do a demonstration," she added.

Alvin hollered, "Noooooooooooo!"